MR. MEN
IN LONDON

Roger Hargreaves

Original concept by
Roger Hargreaves

Written and illustrated by
Adam Hargreaves

EGMONT

D1494449

Mr Busy decided to take all his friends on a trip to London.

Everyone was very excited.

They could not wait to see the sights.

Mr Topsy-Turvy looked at the Tube map to see where they were going to go.

However, Mr Uppity, being the uppity fellow he is, refused to go on the Underground.

Mr Uppity likes to travel alone so he hired a private car to chauffeur him around London.

Which was rather rude of him, but then…

he is the rudest man in the world.

Mr Busy was far too busy to notice.

He and his friends got off the Tube at Covent Garden and began their tour with a visit to the London Transport Museum.

They saw lots of buses and trains.

There were old ones and new ones.

Little Miss Naughty had fun on a bus.

TOOT! TOOT!

Poor Mr Jelly!

After the museum, everyone got back on the Tube to travel to Buckingham Palace.

Little Miss Splendid wanted to see if her house was as splendid as the Queen's.

Mr Tall really is very tall!

Buckingham Palace was very grand, much grander than Little Miss Splendid's house.

Mr Small joined in the changing of the Guard.

Mr Small really is very small!

Then back down to the Underground they all went and Mr Muddle got very muddled on the escalators.

He got his up muddled up with his down.

Or is that his down muddled down with his up?

What a muddle!

They got off the Tube at Leicester Square. Little Miss Giggles loved all the theatres and bright lights.

Mr Noisy liked the lions in Trafalgar Square.

He is as loud as a lion.

Then suddenly Mr Busy ran across the square.

"Look out, Mr Bump!" cried Mr Busy, but it was too late.

Mr Bump had fallen into a fountain.

SPLASH!

On the bus to the Houses of Parliament, Mr Tickle could not resist a tickle.

Or two.

Or three!

And the mischief did not stop there.

At Big Ben, Mr Mischief climbed out onto the clock face and changed the time.

"Tee, hee, hee," he chuckled mischievously to himself.

And Mr Busy, looking up at the clock, thought they were running late.

"Quick, quick!" he called. "Everyone on the boat. Hurry up Mr Slow!"

They sailed down the River Thames and under Tower Bridge.

"What is that?" asked Little Miss Splendid, looking up into the sky. "Is it a bird, is it a plane?"

"No," said Mr Busy. "It's Mr Bounce!"

Just look how high Mr Bounce can bounce.

Finally they reached the Tower of London.

Mr Topsy-Turvy did not get off onto the quay, but he did get off the boat.

sPLASH!

Oh dear.

They had a fascinating tour of the Tower of London.

Mr Strong liked the suits of armour.

Everyone was very impressed.

Everyone, except for Little Miss Splendid.

She did not feel quite so splendid after seeing the Crown Jewels.

And then it was time to go home.

Mr Busy and his friends caught the bus.

It had been a long, Mr Busy busy sort of day and everyone was very tired, but very happy.

Well, not quite everyone.

Everyone except for Mr Uppity who had spent
the day…

…fixing a puncture!